I AM READING

Scaredy Dog!

ANDY ELLIS

KINGFISHER

For Pedro and all the cats

KINGFISHER
First published by Kingfisher 2006
an imprint of Macmillan Children's Books
a division of Macmillan Publishers Limited
20 New Wharf Road, London N1 9RR
Basingstoke and Oxford
www.panmacmillan.com

Associated companies throughout the world

ISBN: 978 0 7534 1362 3

Text and Illustrations copyright © Andy Ellis 2006

The moral right of the author and illustrator has been asserted.

A CIP catalogue record for this book is available from the British Library.

4 6 8 10 9 7 5 3
Printed in China
3TR/1207/WKT/GRS(GRS)/115SEM

Contents

Chapter One

This is Dudley.

Dudley lived with Daphne.

Dudley loved Daphne.

Daphne loved Dudley right back.

Every day, Dudley took Daphne
for a run in the park.
They chased planes and dug for
dinosaur bones.

This tired Daphne out!

Chapter Two

Now, for a dog, Dudley had quite an imagination. For instance, he imagined he wasn't scared of spiders.

But when a spider scuttled across the bedroom floor, it seemed like just the right time to look for lost teddies under the duvet.

"You're a scaredy-dog, Dudley,"
laughed Daphne and she gave him a
hug. "Don't worry, I'll save you!"

Dudley dived back under the duvet. There, in the dark, Dudley couldn't help imagining all the other things that scared him silly!

"There are wasps and bees," Dudley
whispered, "and you can't forget
ghosts and vampires. Oh, and big,
blue, hairy boggles, with googly eyes!"

Of course, Dudley had never actually seen a big, blue, hairy boggle, but that wasn't going to stop him being scared of them.

There was one real scary monster that Dudley didn't have to imagine.

He was a dog called Attila and he was all snarls and pointy teeth.

He lived two doors down, at number forty-eight.

There in the front garden, come rain or shine, was Attila, tied to a tatty, old piece of rope.

Daphne never mentioned Attila.
And she always walked the long way
round to the park, so Dudley didn't
have to go past number forty-eight.

Chapter Three

One day, Dudley and Daphne were watching television when on came a doggy programme.

All the dogs on television were brave and heroic.

Dudley went and looked in the mirror.

Oh dear, Dudley didn't look brave

and heroic.

But then he made a big decision.

Dudley decided he wouldn't be

scared any more.

He would try to be

brave and heroic, like

the dogs on television.

He pressed his nose

to the misty glass.

"Being brave and

heroic can't be

that hard," he

said to himself.

Suddenly, he heard his favourite word.

"Walkies!" cried Daphne.

In the blink of an eye, they were off

down the road towards the park.

When it came to crossing the road, Daphne and Dudley knew just what to do.

"Stop!" said Daphne, "and look . . . and listen . . . and if there are no cars coming, walk briskly across the road, looking and listening as you go."

Daphne smiled at Dudley, but Dudley

didn't notice.

His head was full of daring, doggy

deeds.

21

Chapter Four

They walked through the park gates.
"Come on, Dudley," cried Daphne,
"this looks a likely place to find
dinosaur bones."

But Dudley had other things on his
mind.

"Dudley, the brave and heroic dog, looks around for heroic things to do!" he said to himself.

Suddenly Dudley saw a sweet little girl all alone on a lonely mountain top.

"Dudley, the brave rescue-dog, to the rescue!" he woofed.

But it turned out the sweet little girl didn't need rescuing after all.

She wasn't all that sweet either.

Dudley had only just got his breath
back when he realized he couldn't see
Daphne anywhere.

"Oh dear," thought Dudley, feeling a bit scared.

Then he made another big decision.

"Dudley, the brave and heroic dog, bravely decides to go for a walk on his own."

Then Dudley happened to notice a hoop, for jumping through, like at the circus!

"Dudley, the brave circus-dog, jumps
through the fiery hoop . . . the crowd
gasp!"

But that didn't go well either.

Dudley swung sadly back and forth

in the gentle breeze.

Then he spotted the hot-dog stand.

"Dudley, the brave guard-dog, bravely guards the hot-dogs!"
Dudley's tummy decided it was lunchtime.

Oh dear.

Chapter Five

After a large lunch, Dudley lay in
the daisies and thought some very
big thoughts.

"It's dawned on me," said Dudley to
himself, "that being brave and heroic
isn't very easy at all."

Then he spotted the birds.

"Dudley the sheep-dog bravely rounds
up the flock of sheep . . . er, birds!"
But the birds really didn't want to be
rounded up.

31

Dudley didn't stop running until he was far, far away.

He was feeling very sad.

When he looked at his reflection in a puddle all he saw was a scaredy-dog looking back.

"Dudley, the brave and heroic dog, isn't brave and heroic after all," he said, with a sigh.

"He's just plain, old, scaredy-dog Dudley, just like Daphne said."

"But it would be nice," he thought, as a tear plopped down, "it would be very nice if Daphne was here to give me a hug and a kiss."

Chapter Six

And guess what?

"Dudley!" squeaked Daphne, "I've been looking for you everywhere. I thought you were lost forever!"

She gave him a hug and a kiss. "I love you, you silly old dog," she smiled. And, of course, Dudley loved Daphne right back!

"Come on, let's go home," said Daphne.

They had just got to the park gates
when it started to rain.

Oh dear. Daphne didn't have her

raincoat.

"But it's just a few spots," she said.

Then it was a few more . . . and a few

more . . . and then . . . it was pouring!

"Quick, Dudley, run!" cried Daphne.
And they ran down the street, not

looking where they
were going.
Suddenly, there
was Attila!
They had taken
the wrong way
back home!

Chapter Seven

"ROWWRR!" growled Attila and
he pulled and pulled at the tatty, old
piece of rope.

Pull! . . . Pull! . . . Pull! . . . Pull! . . .
Snap!

The rope broke
and Attila came
charging at them,
with his mean eyes
and his sharp,
pointy teeth.

Daphne was
really scared!
She didn't
know what
to do.

Dudley did.

He stood in front of Daphne, took a

deep breath and . . .

ROOOOOWWWWRRRRR!

It was the loudest growl Daphne had
ever heard.

It was the loudest growl Attila had
ever heard.

It might even have been the loudest
growl in the whole world!

Everything went quiet.

Daphne looked at Dudley.

Dudley didn't look like Dudley.

His fur was all sticking up and he was even fiercer and snarlier than Attila.

Attila took one look at Dudley,
turned tail . . . and ran off!

Chapter Eight

"Dudley, you saved me!" shrieked Daphne and she gave Dudley a hug and a kiss.

"You're not a scaredy-dog any more," she smiled, "you're brave and you're my hero too!" She gave him another hug and a kiss, just in case she hadn't hugged and kissed him enough the first time.

"I love you, Dudley," she said.

And of course, Dudley loved Daphne

right back!

But suddenly . . . Dudley was gone!

"Dudley? Dudley, where are you?"

Unfortunately, just at that moment,

Dudley thought he had spotted a big,

blue, hairy boggle . . .

. . . and he was still scared of those!

About the Author-illustrator

Andy Ellis

This is a portrait of the artist (and writer) as a
rabbit. When he's not a rabbit, Andy likes to
write and illustrate children's books. He also
creates animation series and paints pictures of
landscapes. It was while he was a rabbit that
he met Dudley and Daphne and they told him
this story. "It took a long time," says Andy,
"because rabbits find it quite hard
to hold a pencil."
PS. Don't be scared of spiders. Spiders are
our friends!

Tips for Beginner Readers

1. Think about the cover and the title of the book. What do you think it will be about? While you are reading, think about what might happen next and why.

2. As you read, ask yourself if what you're reading makes sense. If it doesn't, try rereading or look at the pictures for clues.

3. If there is a word that you do not know, look carefully at the letters, sounds, and word parts that you do know. Blend the sounds to read the word. Is this a word you know? Does it make sense in the sentence?

4. Think about the characters, where the story takes place, and the problems the characters in the story faced. What are the important ideas in the beginning, middle and end of the story?

5. Ask yourself questions like:
   Did you like the story?
   Why or why not?
   How did the author make it fun to read?
   How well did you understand it?

Maybe you can understand the story better if you read it again!